MW01240677

UNIT 11

The whole thing began on a warm Thursday morning when I should have been on the school bus heading to my classes. I couldn't be sure exactly where we were going. My parents didn't seem to have a lot to say to me or each other while we were driving along those old country roads. I noticed how they kept glancing back and forth at each other, and then they'd glance at me, but nothing was said. I recall how stone cold and emotionless their faces were. I couldn't begin to imagine what was going through their minds at that very moment. There was no conversation. I had no clue. I just sat in the back seat and stared out the window.

Earlier that morning, they'd ordered me to pack a bag with a couple pairs of pants, shirts, some underwear, a toothbrush and any other stuff that I might need for a short trip. There was no further explanation. I remember how impatient dad was to get on the road.

I thought that was great idea. I was going on a trip with my Mom and Dad and didn't have to go to school that day. I didn't like going to school much anyway. The teachers were bossy and nasty and all the bigger kids bullied me and said mean things about me behind my back. At least, I thought they were talking behind my back. Sometimes, I was certain that one of them said something bad about me but, when I'd turn around, there wasn't even anyone else standing in the room. They must have left quick.

It seemed like we were driving down those dirt roads forever but I guess it was actually only a little under three hours. Dad steered the car down a long and winding driveway lined with some giant oak trees that created a shaded canopy above us. At least, I think they were oaks. Maybe they were elm trees. Oh well, I didn't really care what kind of trees they were anyway. The trees weren't important to my story.

We entered through the enormous black rod-iron gates. I wondered what kind of place it was that we were going to. When I looked out the window, I saw that it had lots of high walls and several red brick buildings surrounded by acres and acres of pastures and dense woods. It looked like no one ever took care of the property. The grass in the common areas was knee high. I looked up and saw that every window in the building had bars on them. Then, I noticed that there was no one walking around outside the red brick buildings and I didn't see even one single person walking around the grounds.

Mom and Dad glanced back and forth at

each other again as Dad parked the car in front of one of the buildings. The entrance of the building had a big sign on it. I read the sign and I knew it spelled out Admissions. It wasn't like any kind of hotel I'd ever seen before.

Wait a minute! I knew that something was wrong. I wasn't feeling too good about the vacation anymore. All at once, I could feel my gut wrenching and a strange feeling came over me. It was a feeling that told me my parents were somehow deceiving me … lying to me, but I didn't say anything. What could I say?

Dad opened the trunk of the car and dropped my suitcase on the ground in front of me. Wait a minute! Where was their luggage? The trunk was empty. I didn't see anything they'd packed. Mom opened her car door, got out and glanced around at the buildings and the grounds. She turned to my father and said, "We're here, Jonah. It looks so cold from the outside."

Dad slapped his hands on his hips and said, "What did you expect? Let's just go inside and get this over with."

I turned to them and asked, sounding a bit desperate, "Mom, Dad, what is this place? Why are we here?"

Mom just smiled at me uncomfortably. Then, she turned to dad and gave him the same smile. It wasn't a smile of happiness. It was a smile of uncertainty. I could see she was holding back her tears. I wasn't sure why she felt the need to be so sad. Come to think of it, dad had that exact same forced smile on his face. I didn't know what was going on or why we were there but I stopped asking questions.

I picked up my heavy overpacked suitcase with both hands and gradually dragged it up the walkway, following behind my parents. My father didn't offer to help me carry the suitcase.

•

We entered the admissions building. Inside, I noticed there was a big metal desk to the left with a huge glass half-wall in front of it. Everything about its appearance was beginning to tell me it was a hospital.

Wait a minute! A hospital? What was wrong with me? Was I sick and didn't even know it? My parents could see it was all gradually unfolding in my mind. I became guarded. I wanted to know what was going on.

Dad walked up to the desk to speak to the husky gray-haired woman behind the clear glass panel. She was wearing white pants, a dark blue smock and a nametag that read Greta. After glancing at her nametag, Dad said, "Hello, Greta. I'm Jonah Skinner and this is my wife Helen. We have our son Marvin here. Your doctor should be expecting us".

Nurse Greta pulled out a stack of papers and asked my parents to sign and/or initial each one of them. She thumbed through them to make sure they were all there. I watched Dad flip through each of the forms on the clipboard, hardly bothering to read them before he signed them. The woman didn't even crack a smile as she made sure he had signed every page. She announced, "Alright, Mr. Skinner. Everything seems to be in order here. I'll call Dr. Dunlap. He should be right down."

Dad nodded his head and stood there. He was waiting for further instructions.

Greta pointed over at the waiting area and said, "Why don't you have a seat over there until he gets here?" Dad glanced over and saw the orange plastic waiting room chairs. I noticed half the chairs in the room were old and cracked. Even I could see that they needed to be repaired or replaced. Oh well, not my problem.

Mom and dad sat where the receptionist had pointed to. Mom picked up one of the magazines from the table in front of her. I think it was a food magazine. She pretended to read it but I could tell that she wasn't able to concentrate very well. She simply flipped through the pages, glancing at them quickly, staring at the pictures, looking around the waiting area and then flipping to another page. Dad did the same, pushing the magazines around on the table until he found one that dealt with fishing or sports cars or baseball.

I saw that the walls inside the building were all painted a pale-yellow color. I noticed there was a set of elevators at the end of the lengthy and vacant hallway.

I kept looking back at the husky woman behind the glass. She seemed to be so lost in her paperwork, that she never even picked her head up once or bothered to ask us if we needed anything. It felt as if we were waiting there for a long, long time. My parents remained silent. Then, I had to do it. I opened my mouth and blurted, "What's wrong with me?"

Mom and Dad stopped doing what they were doing and glanced at each other for a brief moment. I sat and waited for one of them to answer me, but they just paged through their magazines again, ignoring me. Neither one replied, so, I let it drop for now. I figured I'd find out soon enough, but it must have been bad since none of my brothers or sisters were there. What was wrong with me that wasn't wrong with them? Did I need an operation or something?

By the time the doctor arrived, mom had gone through at least six of the magazines that were originally fanned out on the coffee table. The doctor came out of the elevator. His shoes were heavy. I could hear clomp, clomp, clomp as he made his way down the hallway.

He looked like a typical doctor, tall, slim, little round glasses, thinning gray hair, wrinkled button-down shirt and a long white smock. Like I said. It was the typical doctor look, like the doctor's I'd see on tv.

As he marched towards the waiting area, I noticed he was holding a manila folder that he occasionally peered into as needed. When Mom and Dad saw him coming, they immediately set their magazines down on the table and sat upright. They sat at attention like he was their army commander or something.

When he entered the waiting area, Mom and Dad stood up and the introductions began. "Mr. and Mrs. Skinner, I'm Dr. Randall Dunlap. I'm truly sorry that we have to meet under these unfortunate circumstances." He glanced down at me and said, "And this must be your son Marvin."

He shook my hand but I wasn't going to say a word until I knew what was going on. Then, he turned his attention to my parents again when he apologized, "I'm very sorry about the long wait. We were having a bit of a problem upstairs in Unit 3 but it appears that the situation has been resolved and is under control for the moment."

There was a pause of silence as the doctor glanced at Greta and then into his folder one more time. "Why don't we go upstairs to my office where we can speak more candidly?"

My parents nodded. They looked at me and said with their eyes, "Get out of the chair. Let's go, Marvin."

We proceeded down the long pale-yellow hallway to those creaky metal elevators. I noticed Dr. Dunlap put a key in the metal keyhole on the wall to make the doors open. I always thought you just had to push the buttons. No one spoke during the assent. The doctor, once again, looked into the folder. My parents stared up at the ceiling as if the doctor's office would suddenly appear if they stared hard enough. The elevator moved slowly. It took a while but the doors eventually opened and everyone unloaded to destinations unknown.

The doctor shuffled the folder from hand to hand as we traveled down another pale-yellow hallway. His shoes still making that clomp, clomp sound. I was getting a weird feeling in the pit of my stomach. Wait. Who said that? I thought someone said something to me, but no one did. There was nobody else in the hallway. I always hated when those things would happen.

Dr. Dunlap led us into a sad and depressing room. The name on the gold door plaque read Dr. Randall Dunlap. The office was small and cramped and it smelled like mold or some kind of old rotting food. He extended his arm out to guide us in. I saw a desk covered with folders and notepads, two tall, gray file cabinets, a bookshelf loaded with books of all sizes, shapes and colors and a dying plant sitting on the grimy windowsill beneath a filthy window that was protected with prison bars.

Dr. Dunlap sat behind the desk and tossed the folder on top of the rest. He said, "Please, have a seat and we can get started." Everyone sat down at the exact same time. Perhaps I wasn't the only one that had a weird feeling in the pit of my stomach. I was hoping I'd find out why I was there soon. I had to know what was wrong with me.

The doctor began asking a series of normal questions to my parents. Most of the inquiries made very little sense to me at the time. "And how old is Marvin?"

Dad was the first to answer. "He's thirteen, Dr. Dunlap. He'll be turning fourteen in a couple of months."

Mom added, "He was born in August of nineteen sixty-three."

The doctor questioned, "Are there any other

children that are living in the house or is he the only child presently there?"

Dad said, "He's the youngest of our six children. Most of them are still living at home right now. Our oldest daughter's getting married in a few months, so she'll be leaving … and you know the rest of the situation."

The doctor nodded and peered back into that folder. For some unknown reason, Mom declared, "I had three girls and three boys. He was the last one, the baby."

Thanks mom, I think the doctor would have figured that out since dad said all my siblings were older than me. Why does she always have to put in her two cents when no one asked her to? It really bugs me. Sometimes, I think she just likes to hear the sound of her own voice.

Dunlap continued, "Do any of his brothers or sisters deal with a similar problem, either now or in the past?"

Dad blurted, "Nope. Not that we know of … just Marvin. The others are fine."

Mom interrupted with, "Well, don't you remember that time Jeannie ran away when she was only fourteen?"

Dad tried to explain. "I don't think that's what the doctor was asking us, Helen."

"No?"

"Besides, she was only gone for a total of four hours and we found her at her best friend's house that night. She was there the whole time. It's not the same thing."

The doctor agreed with dad. "He's correct, Mrs. Skinner. I wasn't asking about the normal childhood rebellion."

She hung her head and apologized, "I'm sorry, doctor."

He nodded before he continued. "How long ago did you first begin to notice little Marvin's symptoms?"

I thought about what he asked. What symptoms was he talking about? I feel fine. At least, I think I feel fine. Do I? Sure, I do. I mean … I thought I did.

But Dr. Dunlap just kept going on and on with the never-ending questions. "Has he ever had any other type of a psychiatric evaluation done on him in the past?"

Again, Dad was the first one to answer the question. He responded, "No, this is the first time we've ever actually done something like this. There have been discussions with others but none of them were this extreme. Up until now, we didn't know what to do with the boy. You never know about this stuff until someone else tells you what to do. We only know that it has to be done. We're at the end of our rope."

Wait a minute, psychiatric evaluation? Dr. Dunlap was a psychiatrist? That's what this was all about. They all think I'm crazy. I shot up from my chair and announced, "Mom! Dad! I'm not crazy!" Defensively, I began to back up across the room. Everyone else stood up appearing self-protective as if I was going to lose my cool and try something stupid. Once again, I shouted, "Mom! Dad! I told you! I'm not crazy!"

Mom smiled at me nervously and said, "Of course you're not crazy, honey. No one said that you were. We're just here to help you the best way we can."

Mom, Dad and Dr. Dunlap all tried to say things they thought would help to calm me down … but I was calm. At least I thought I was calm at the time. Mom, with that overly-concerned look in her eyes, said, "Marvin, please try to understand this is for your own good. No one's here to hurt you. We just want to get our lives back to normal. We want you to be taken care of."

Dad sternly ordered, "Son, come over here and sit back down. They're going to take good care of you here."

I began to find it disturbing when the doctor mumbled something about something that he called Thora … Thorazine … whatever that was. I yelled and clinched my fists. "Alright! Alright! I'll sit back down!" I had to listen to them or they'd think that I really was out of my head.

When all was calm again, in that murky office, the doctor, with a pen in hand, sat erect in his chair, made eye contact with me and stated, "I have an idea. Why don't I call one of the nurses to come and give you a little tour of the place … to see what you think?"

I just shrugged my shoulders. What else could I do? I didn't want to go but I didn't want to have another outburst either.

He added, "Besides, your mother and father can answer the rest of the questions that I have. And later on, you can come back in here and we'll have a talk, just the two of us … man to man." Then he winked. He was a creepy guy.

What could I say? I realized I had to do what he said or they most likely would've dragged me away. I watched as Dr. Dunlap picked up the phone and pushed the number seven button on the keypad. He said, "Could you send Nurse Lisa down to meet with Marvin Skinner. I'd like her to give him a tour of the facility. Okay. Thank you."

He laid the phone back in its cradle and said, "Nurse Lisa will be right down. She's just finishing up with another patient."

Oh great, another aging nurse. I was praying

that she didn't look like that outdated creature at the admissions desk that I met with earlier. But maybe the one at the front desk was the best looking one they had. After all, why would a beautiful woman want to work in a dismal place like that? But … I could still hope.

We sat there silently and the doctor tapped the top of his pen on the desk as we waited. He kept glancing down at that stupid file on top of the stack … my file, my damned file. I wondered what he had written in that file. What the hell did I do to end up in this place?

I wasn't crazy. I know I wasn't. Crazy was that old lady downtown that was missing all of her teeth. She smelled like she never took a bath. She just pushed a shopping cart around the streets, all day and night. It was a shopping cart that was full of garbage. She just walked around with her head hung down all the time and she never spoke to anyone. I couldn't even walk by her because she smelled so bad. She was gross.

Crazy was that old guy with the bloodshot eyes and red nose that was always drunk, sitting outside O'Malley's Tavern. And when he ran out of money for booze and was too smashed to make it home, he'd pass out in the dark alley out behind the bar and stay there all night.

Crazy were those kids that lived on the other

side of town. Mom explained to me that they had something called Downs Syndrome. I wondered how they ever got that way. Were they in some kind of an accident or were they born like that? That's crazy. That wasn't me. I was normal. I wasn't nuts. I couldn't understand why they were doing that to me. Didn't they want me anymore? Didn't they love me? I wasn't crazy.

There was an abrupt knock on the office door. Everyone's eyes turned to the door. The doctor cheerfully said, "Come in, Lisa. I want you to meet Marvin."

I almost fell off my chair when I saw that beautiful woman enter the room. I think my jaw might have hit the floor. Wow! She wasn't just beautiful. She was gorgeous.

Dr. Dunlap said, "Marvin, this is Nurse Lisa. She's been working here with us for over five years and she'll be showing you around some of the hospital today. I particularly want her to show you Unit 3. I'm going to remain here with your parents so we can talk some more about your file. I'll see you later on for that man to man talk I mentioned." He winked again.

Nurse Lisa smelled so fresh and fragrant. I could tell she wasn't wearing some cheap perfume. She must've been wearing the best stuff there was … something from Paris. She was so sweet as she

guided me out of Dunlap's office and into the rest
of the building that I didn't even say "Goodbye" to
my parents or the doctor.

After another bouncy elevator trip, we got
out on the third floor. And again, there was another
pale-yellow hallway of pure emptiness. What was
up with this place? Couldn't someone even hang a
picture on a wall around here?

Lisa perfume smelled so nice. I don't think I
ever smelled anything that nice before. And she was
so beautiful. She was gorgeous. I think I might have
already said that. Her hair was long and blonde and
shiny. She didn't look like the rest of the women in
that depressing place. All the other nurses looked
like fat old cows. They were glum and unhappy and
overweight. Each one of them was jam-packed with
bad attitudes and a ham sandwich. They didn't need
the ham sandwich.

We walked up to two big metal doors at the
end of the hallway. Lisa took a set of keys from her
pocket to open the doors. As they opened, she said,
"Marvin, this is called the locked unit. This is where
all the new children stay when they're first admitted
to this institution. Eventually, you'll be moved to
another floor or another building … most likely it'll
be Unit 11."

Wait a minute! Eventually? How long were

they planning on keeping me in this hellhole? This was going to ruin my whole summer vacation if I was going to be stuck there for more than a couple of weeks. After all, school was going to be over in just thirteen days. Then I'd have three months of fun, and … I did make some plans with some kids that lived on the next block.

The doors opened with a heavy clanging sound. The unit looked sort of like a hospital but not exactly. Lisa pointed at a dimly lit room that was furnished with a desk and a couple file cabinets. It had a sliding glass window just like the admissions desk had. Lisa told me, "This is the nurse's station. You're never allowed to enter this room. This is for the nurses and orderlies only."

I saw that the long hallway in front of me had twelve doors, six on each side. She pointed to a big room in the other direction and said, "This is the community recreation area. It's a place for you and the other children come and relax. We even have a television in there."

Then, she pointed towards a couple other large pale-yellow rooms. "The group meeting room and the arts and crafts room are over there … off to the side."

She pointed her finger towards that long hallway as she explained, "Those first ten doors are the patient rooms. When we have full occupancy there's two children to a room. Right now, our population is low. So, you'll most likely get some extra special attention."

Lisa smiled at me. Her eyes were a beautiful deep shade of blue. Her eyes almost made me forget that I was being forced to walk around this pale-yellow hellhole. She continued. "The rooms on the right side are for the girls and the rooms on the left are for the boys. Your room will be the fifth door on the left, down near the end of the hall, and you'll have a roommate."

Hold on! Wait a minute! Who ever said I was planning to stay there? I never agreed to that! I thought it was just a tour of the unit. I turned and noticed a dark-haired nurse seated in the nurse's station. She was a lot older than Lisa, but she seemed friendly enough.

She was talking with a man. He was a tall man with big arms and a broad chest. I didn't know exactly who it was at the time. But then I found out that he was one of the orderlies who worked the graveyard shift. I thought I heard him tell the nurse that he just stopped by to pick up his paycheck. His eye caught me standing in the hallway, staring at him, but he didn't come out or bother to say hello or even crack a smile.

Lisa checked the polish on her soft-pink fingernails as she explained, "We only have seven patients on the unit right now. You'll be number eight and I'm sure more will follow soon enough. Everyone on the floor is between ten and fourteen years old … around your age. You should get along with them."

That didn't make any sense when she said that. Just because someone's the same age as me, doesn't mean that we're going to automatically get along with each other. If that was the case, I would have been best friends with all of my classmates back in school.

Lisa still took it upon herself to assume that I was staying when it all could've changed in the blink of an eye. Perhaps my parents would realize they couldn't live without me in the house and tell Dr. Dunlap that they changed their minds. Perhaps the doctor would tell my parents they're crazy and decide to keep them there instead of me. Perhaps. Perhaps. It was always a guessing game with places like that. Perhaps. Perhaps. Perhaps.

We continued our tour down the hallway and into the patient's rooms. I saw that dark-haired nurse and the orderly continuing to chat some stupid gossip as if I wasn't even there.

Lisa and I walked into a room. It was the fifth door at the end of the hall. It was the room that Lisa declared would be my new home for a while. I saw a young boy laying on one of the two beds. He appeared to be sleeping. I noticed that there wasn't much furniture in the room, two beds, a closet, two nightstands and a dresser. The floor was white tile with no carpeting. That was it. No telephone. No television or radio.

Lisa whispered, "That young man on the bed is Timmy. He's asleep right now but you can get to know him later, when he wakes up. I'm sure you'll end up best friends before you know it."

There she goes again, thinking I'm going to be friends with someone just because were the same age. She kept assuming I was going to stay there for some reason. She assumed wrong. "This is going to be your room and Timmy is going to be your new roommate. The boy's bathroom is just next door. Try not to mix it up with the girl's bathroom on the other side of the hall."

Lisa explained, "You'll most likely be on a schedule to attend certain groups that meet each day at specific times. It's expected."

She didn't get into much detail about the certain groups but that was fine with me, providing it wasn't going to be for very long. I didn't plan to stay here and ruin my summer vacation and I wasn't really interested in hearing about the stupid groups anyway.

She told me we'd get one hour of television each day. Wow! What a treat! Not a whole hour of television. What a vacation!

While we were talking, a girl came out of one of the right-side rooms. She looked like a ten-year-old zombie from a horror movie. Her head was hung down and she wasn't really walking. It was more like she was shuffling out of her door. Lisa said, "Marvin, this is Charlotte."

Charlotte gradually shuffled her way over to me and lifted her head. As she stared at me, I noticed she looked tired, weak and confused. Her eyes had dark circles under them and her blonde greasy hair looked as if it hadn't been washed or combed in a week.

She was wearing pink pajamas, covered with a bathrobe, and fuzzy pink slippers. She was holding an old brown teddy bear that was missing one of its black-button eyes.

As she lifted her head, she put her hand out and whispered with no emotion, almost robotically, "Hello, Marvin. Welcome to the Providence State Asylum for Children."

Then, she dropped her head down again and shuffled back towards the hall to the bathroom on the girls' side of the hall. I looked around the area and then I glanced back at Lisa and said, "It sure is quiet in here."

Lisa responded, "Sometimes, but then other times it's a madhouse in here. It can get very noisy when we have full occupancy."

Time seemed to pass quickly while I was talking to Lisa. The desk nurse with the dark hair was named Diane. I read her nametag.

She came over to us and said, "Dr. Dunlap is ready to see Marvin again."

Lisa looked towards the big metal entrance doors and asked, "Shall we?" as she guided me back out of the unit and down to the rickety elevator to another pale-yellow hallway.

We got back to the Dr. Dunlap's office and I noticed my parents weren't there anymore. I guess I looked a little shocked when I realized that. Maybe they just stepped out front for a minute to smoke a cigarette or talk in private.

Dr. Dunlap caringly said, "Marvin, I'm sorry to tell you that your parents have gone home for the day. They answered all the questions I needed from them and signed the remainder of the necessary commitment paperwork. Then, they said they had to leave."

They just left me there? But they never even bothered to say goodbye to me. How could they have done that to me? How could they have been so cold and heartless? After all, I was their baby boy. Lisa assured me, "I'm sure they'll be back to visit you very soon, Marvin."

I supposed this meant I was stuck there …
but I didn't want to stay in that place with the pale-
yellow walls, the dingy white tile floors and the
windows that were so dirty I couldn't see outside of
them.

Lisa smiled at me sympathetically before
she told the doctor she'd be upstairs in Unit 3 if he
needed her for anything else. She put her hand on
my shoulder and gave me another compassionate
smile just before she exited the room. "I'll see you
on the third floor in a little while, Marvin. You take
care of yourself."

The doctor let out a heavy breath, grinned a
big grin, and said, "Why don't you have a seat so
we can have that man to man chat I mentioned." He
winked at me again. Did this guy think it made him
cool to wink at me?

I did as he said. After all, it seemed that I
didn't have much of a choice. I sat in the cold chair
at the front of his desk, still in shock that mom and
dad had just left without even one word to me. And
Dunlap still had that damned folder on his desk in
front of him. He asked, "Do you think you're up to
answering a few questions for me, Marvin? I have
quite a list here."

I agreed. He stated, "Why don't we start by
you telling me a little bit about yourself and why
you think you're here today."

I told him I was thirteen and in the eighth grade. He already knew I had five older brothers and sisters. I didn't know what other information he wanted to know. He questioned, "Do you get along with all of your brothers and sisters?"

That was a real stupid question. Of course, I didn't. We were brothers and sisters. I let him know that I'd fight with my brother Kent a lot … all the time … every day. It's always been a never-ending feud for control between the two of us for as long as I could remember.

He asked, "Why do you think you fight with your brother Kent so often?"

Dr. Dunlap was really piling on the deep questions. I told him our fights happened because Kent was three years older than me and he always acted like he was my boss. I hated it when he tried to tell me what to do. Dunlap inquired, "And tell me, Marvin, exactly how bad do the fights between the two of you get?"

I lied when I told him the fights weren't that bad. I didn't want to tell him just how severe they actually escalated to … like the time I took the mirror off the wall and smashed it over his head. He had to get twenty-eight stitches. Why would I have to take the blame for it. It wasn't my fault. After all, he started the fight. He made me so mad that day that all I saw was rage.

And then there was the time I put that steak knife up to his throat for almost twenty minutes. I never cut him but, God, he was so scared, he cried while I laughed.

"Do you get along with the other classmates in your school?"

I guess I did. I never really thought about it that much. I just wasn't in the mood to talk about the few incidents that happened there. Besides, everybody in school gets into fights. Isn't that a normal part of a kid's life?

He probed, "Do you ever hear little voices in your head commanding you to do the things that you follow through with, things that you normally wouldn't do otherwise?"

How did he know about the voices? I never told anyone about that. I mumbled, "Yes. Once in a while … I guess."

"Tell me what kinds of things do they tell you to do."

I can't believe he really wanted to talk about those stupid voices. I never talked about the voices with anyone. He calmly said, "Just take your time, Marvin. It's just the two of us here right now. No one else can hear you. You can be honest and tell me what they say to you. I'm not here to judge. I'm here to help." Can you believe the guy winked at me again?

God! I didn't want to talk about those damned voices but he persisted over and over. So, I was just going to spit it out. "Okay! They tell me to do things to other people. They tell me which people aren't nice, the ones who talk about me behind my back and make fun of me all the time, like my brother Kent. They say that I should hurt them before they hurt me."

Dunlap continued, "And do you always act on it when the voices are commanding you to do these things?"

Suddenly, I could feel my face and body getting warmer. I felt angry and trapped like I was in a cage. I just wanted to get out of that freaking office! Who did this guy think he was ... talking about things he had no control over ... things I had no control over? I shouted, "Yes! Yes! I always do what they tell me to do or they don't stop! It's the only way I can get them to go away! The voices keep going on and on and on!"

There was a pause, a silent moment. It gave me time to cool down a little. I believed it gave him time to come up with more stupid questions. He opened that damned file and peered into it again before he asked, "Tell me, Marvin. How often do you hear these voices in your head?"

"How often? I don't know."

"Do you hear them once a week or every

day or several times a day?"

I just wanted the conversation to end. I bellowed, "I don't really know. It's different all the time. It always changes."

Suddenly, his deep, monotone voice got a little more demanding. It was as if he was as tired of asking me the questions as I was answering them. "How often do you hear the voices? Be honest with me, Marvin. It's the only way I can help you get rid of them for good."

I didn't want to answer any more of his senseless questions. "Every day. I hear them every day!" I couldn't believe I blurted that out without even thinking first.

The doctor walked around the desk and stood in front of me. "Do you want me to help you learn to deal with this problem? It's ultimately going to be your choice. Maybe I can help you learn to live with these voices and you controlling them instead of them controlling you."

He seemed very reassuring. I guess I trusted him a little. What else was I going to do since my parents dropped me off at the door and hightailed it out of there. I had no other choice but to trust him. I expressed, "Yes, I think so. I'd like you to help me, Dr. Dunlap."

Dr. Dunlap smiled, rubbed my shoulder and said, "That's good. I think we're off to a great start,

Marvin. I hope you realize that was the first step in getting better."

For hours, we discussed my parents and my siblings, the voices, my school and other things that ended up making me feel very uncomfortable. Dr. Dunlap already knew about the steak knife and broken mirror incident. It was all right there in that stupid file on the desk. How much more was he planning to drill out of my head?

We talked about the two pet hamsters that I killed. I told him that they were sick and I couldn't stand to see them suffering anymore. No animal should have to suffer. They had to be put out of their misery. And there was a rabbit I found and our dog, Clover. I didn't mean to kill him. I told mom and dad it was an accident … and that was over three years before anyway.

Soon enough, we moved onto a different topic. He wanted to know about my history of starting fires. I mean, I never burned a building down or anything like that. They were only small fires, but I knew other kids that started fires too. I thought that was just part of being a kid. I didn't see any of them in an asylum. I didn't see any of them in Unit 3.

I was getting really tired. Dunlap's clock made me aware of the fact that it was three o'clock in the afternoon. I was hungry. I was starving! I hadn't eaten anything since six-thirty that morning. But we talked and talked and talked. I stared at the clock. Three-thirty, three-forty-five, four o'clock, four-fifteen.

Finally! He announced, "Well, I think we can wrap it up for today, Marvin. Besides, you must be quite hungry by now."

Gee, what a brilliant observation, Dunlap. I can't believe I didn't get a wink for that comment. I replied, "Yeah, a little."

He added, "And as for your new medication regiment, we're going to be starting you on a low dose of Thorazine four times a day at 7am, noon, 5pm and 10pm. The nurses will make sure you take your medication and that they're administered at the correct times. Alright, Marvin?"

I got loud. "Yeah!" I had to agree with him since I had no other choice but to comply with his crazy demands.

He picked up his phone and hit the button for Unit 3 again. "Yes, Lisa, he's ready to go back upstairs. No, he's not giving me any trouble. He's been quite compliant."

Lisa came back to his office to take me and my suitcase up to Unit 3. Before we left, Dr. Dunlap briefed her on the new medication, the dosages, the times, and several other things.

Then, they stood on the other side of the

room, whispering to each other, and occasionally glancing my way. He handed her some paperwork and her very own folder that she could look into, and we were on our way.

Dunlap told me that he'd be seeing me every day during the week from ten to eleven in the morning. Great, what an excellent summer vacation I was having. Then, he patted me on the back and winked at me one more time. I knew there would have to be at least one more wink before I left with Lisa and the suitcase.

For the next couple weeks, I met with Dr. Dunlap each day as scheduled and complied with the wishes of nurses Lisa and Diane ... and even with that graveyard shift orderly whose name turned out to be Carl. There were a few other nurses and orderlies in the unit but I never had much to do with them. They seemed to be more like shadows instead of real people to me.

Carl was a questionable character ... sort of strange... very intimidating. He looked as if he spent all his days lifting weights in the gym but probably couldn't spell his own first name correctly. I don't know why, but I didn't trust him. I didn't trust him one iota. Something in my gut told me that guy was nothing but trouble.

I took the medications that the nurses told

me to take, when they told me to take them and how they told me to take them, even though they made me feel muddled and disoriented. I attended their long and boring groups and classes that they had arranged for me. Believe it or not, I even raised my hand and answered questions a few times. I just wanted to get out!

I remember walking the halls every day, back and forth and back and forth. Eventually, I noticed I was shuffling, like Charlotte, instead of walking. I realized that the Thorazine was changing everything … my mood, my thoughts, and even the way I walked down the hallways. I was always so tired and weak.

One particular evening, a loud crash woke me up from a sound sleep. When I sat up, I saw Timmy's dark silhouette sitting up in his bed too. I asked, "What the hell was that noise, Timmy? It sounded like thunder."

Timmy shook his head, "I'm not sure what it was but I hope it's not Harry again."

I had no idea what he meant by that. "Harry? What's wrong with Harry?"

Then, we heard a second crash and Timmy whispered, "Harry stopped taking his meds a few times. Whenever he does that, he goes off, out of control and gets destructive."

I got out of my bed and crept towards the door. In a quiet, panicked tone, Timmy questioned, "Where are you going, Marvin?"

I didn't respond to him as I stepped softly on the white tile floor. Besides, Timmy knew exactly where I was going.

"Get back in your bed before Carl comes in here and catches you."

I ignored Timmy's request and slowly opened the door a few inches until I could see clearly down the hallway and the common area. I spotted Carl and Diane running in circles near the nurse's desk. Then, I saw Harry racing around and ducking to avoid being caught. When he was off his meds, Harry was quick.

Timmy inquired, "What do you see out there, Marvin?"

Again, I didn't answer. That's when I heard another crash. Harry kept throwing himself off the walls, knocking trays over, and kicking the plastic chairs around. Carl and Diane looked completely frustrated and angry. Harry didn't stop. He seemed to be channeling all the energy those medications had been bringing to a standstill. Even I could see that he was out of control.

I saw that Carl finally caught Harry when he grabbed him by the upper arm. Then, Diane held his kicking feet and they carried him off to a room that was located behind the nurse's station. It was a room I never noticed before.

I saw that Charlotte's bedroom door was opened a tiny bit too. She must have been just as curious as I was. We waited for almost an hour for Carl and Diane to come back out of the room with Harry. Eventually, I saw Charlotte's door close. I took her lead and went back to bed. I noticed that Timmy had already lost interest and fallen back to sleep.

It was just another day sitting in the pale-yellow rec room, eating our lunches. All the other kids were whispering about the night before. I guess me and Charlotte weren't the only ones peeking out from out rooms.

Anita, the cubby girl who always had a book in her hand, leaned over and whispered to Andrew, "Did you hear all the commotion last night? I guess Harry was out of control again."

Andrew, who had a little crush on Paulette, Anita's roommate, leaned in a whispered, "He was making a lot of noise last night. He sure must have given Carl a run for his money."

Paulette, the snooty know-it-all, folded her arms on the table and announced, "Harry's always causing trouble in this unit. If you ask me, he should be put in one of the bad units."

I watched as Evan, Rick and even Charlotte got in on the conversation. Timmy and I just sat there and watched how they gossiped back and forth to each other. I thought that they were acting worse than adults acted when they gossiped. Abruptly, I said, "Shut up. Just shut up."

Everyone stopped talking at once and then they just stared at me, waiting for me to say what I wanted to say. "I don't think we should be talking bad about Harry. I mean, he's not even here to defend himself."

Timmy mentioned, "Yeah, where is Harry anyway? He wasn't in his room this morning. What did they do with him?"

Paulette spoke up again. "Like I was saying, Harry's always been a problem with his outbursts. I think they moved him to another unit, or maybe he's in timeout somewhere." Then, Paulette stood up from the table, grabbed her lunch tray, stuck her nose in the air and walked out. Of course, Andrew got up and followed her out.

Rick and Evan continued to question the whereabouts of Harry. I let it go for now. Lisa popped her head in the door and said, "Make sure everyone cleans up after themselves today. I'm not your maid."

Timmy and I decided to go back to our room and nap a bit before dinner. He wanted to talk about

Harry with me and I wanted to talk about Harry with him, but we never did.

The last time we saw Harry was when he was being taken to that room behind the nurses' station. I kept a watchful eye on the door to that room every time I walked by.

No one had seen Harry in days though we all knew, deep inside, that he was still in the room behind the nurse's station. I watched Dr. Dunlap make frequent visit's there along with the nurses and the orderlies.

I recall the Friday that Harry was finally brought out from the room. One of the daytime nurses, Noreen, gathered all seven children from the ward together in the meeting room. She alerted us that Harry would be a little different than the last time we saw him. I didn't know what that meant. She commented, "Since Harry was so against taking his medications orally, Dr. Dunlap ordered that they be given to him by injection, and the doctor also increased his dosage."

We watched in horror as Harry was brought out of the secret room in a wheelchair. His head was hung to the side and with his mouth wide open and his tongue hanging out, drool streamed out the side and down onto his shoulder. I noticed his eyes just stared up at the ceiling with little to no blinking. He looked like a vegetable.

Noreen remarked, "Harry won't be giving any of us and more problems. It's all been taken care of. His days of spur-of-the-moment outbursts are finished."

From then on, it seemed Harry would live the rest of his life out in that wheelchair, heavily medicated and wearing diapers. He was completely unaware of everyone and everything around him. It was all taken away from him in one night, his life and his dignity.

As time moved forward, I got to be a little friendlier with my roommate Timmy and a couple of the other guys in the unit. I noticed they all slept a lot. As a matter of fact, everyone on Unit 3 slept a lot, including me. It must have been those damned meds that they were forcing down out throats, but we had to take the meds or, I was sure, we'd end up like Harry.

The food was almost edible most of the time but it wasn't even close to my mother's great home cooking. Speaking of Mom and Dad, they still hadn't come back to visit me … no cards, no letters, no phone calls, nothing … not a word. Nothing from my parents, or my brothers or even my sisters. I thought I would've heard from somebody by then. After all, they were my whole world. At least, I thought they were my whole world. Unit 3 was not my whole world.

Dr. Dunlap talked to me endlessly but I wasn't really feeling any different. His monotone words would just go on and on and on like static on a radio station. The voices were still there. They were still telling me things that I should do. They wanted me to do bad things to Carl and Nurse Diane. But, surprisingly, I wasn't acting on them. I guess that's because my brain was so scrambled up from all the freaking medications, and I didn't have the energy to follow through.

Some days were much more difficult than others. It was that one day in early June when I met with the doctor in that drab office. He greeted me as he typically did. "Good morning, Marvin. I hope that you're feeling well today." Then, I'd get that stupid wink.

As always, I simply shrugged my shoulders and bowed my head but didn't respond. "Why don't you have a seat?"

I flopped in the chair and, after letting out a prolonged breath, responded, "Okay, Dr. Dunlap. I'm in the chair."

As usual, he said, "I hope everything's been going well for you in Unit 3." What could I say? I was feeling like a zombie most of the time. How the hell did I know how things were actually going? No one ever told me if I was making progress or if I wasn't making progress.

He asked me if I wanted something to drink as he walked to his water cooler and filled up a cup for himself.

Politely, I answered, "No, thank you, Dr. Dunlap. I just had some water with breakfast before I came in."

For some reason his conversation, that day, revolved around my oldest brother, Christopher. He was the sibling that was six years older than me. He asked about how close I was to him. I didn't know quite what he was getting at.

I thought about Christopher but I couldn't answer. I didn't really have many memories of him. After all, he was a lot older than me. It's not like we grew up together or even spent any quality time together. He hung out with his teenage friends and I usually stayed away from them. I didn't like the fact that they drank alcohol and smoked cigarettes. They even tried to get me to did it a few times. I knew it was bad for me and I refused.

I tried to think about Christopher. The meds had me so confused, how could I remember my brother? Those damned meds were wiping out my memories. What did Dr. Dunlap expect from me? But would I have remembered Christopher and those things a few weeks ago when I wasn't nailed down on their drugs?

It was around that time that I changed the subject and asked him the question, "Where are my parents?"

Dr. Dunlap seemed surprised that I'd even bring them up. "Your parents?"

"Yes, my parents. Why haven't I heard a word from either of them?"

The doctor quickly answered, "Well, I just spoke to your parents yesterday, Marvin. They said they've been very busy at home and couldn't find the time to make the long drive out here. They were sure you'd understand."

I was utterly shocked that he had spoken to Mom and Dad but had never planned to tell me about the conversation unless I brought it up first. I didn't want to cooperate with him anymore. He was a liar.

I don't know what exactly made me feel the way I did that day. It was just a gut feeling. How could he hold back such important information? It was then that I began to mistrust Dr. Dunlap. He wanted me to share all my thoughts and personal feelings but he couldn't even share the fact that my parents had called.

"Oh my God! Help me! Someone! Help

me!" I remember waking up one night, screaming out, and tossing and turning violently in my bed. My t-shirt was drenched in sweat and my hands wouldn't stop trembling. Carl, the creepy orderly, and my roommate Timmy said that I was as white as a ghost.

When it finally stopped and I had a moment to collect myself and catch my breath, Nurse Diane brought me a plastic cup of water. Timmy asked me what it was that had me so terrified. I answered, "I-I think I had a horrible nightmare but I don't have a clue what it was about. I can't remember any of it except for blood. I saw lots of blood."

I saw little Charlotte standing outside the door of my room holding that beat up old teddy bear in her arms. Her skin looked almost as pale as mine did. I'm sure my screaming must have frightened her too.

Carl noticed her lurching out there in the hallway. Hastily, he slapped his thigh and pointed his finger toward her bedroom door. It was as if he was commanding some kind of trained dog. "Go, Charlotte! Back to bed! Now!" Immediately, she turned and shuffled back into her room, dragging her bear along.

After a few minutes and a few sips of water, I calmed down. I was surprised that Carl and Diane had left the room and never bothered to ask why I was so terrified. It was as if they only cared that the unit was quiet again.

Carl was the last one out of the room. Before he left, he glanced, with a malicious grin, at Timmy and then me. I believe that was the first time that I heard Carl threaten me. From outside our bedroom door, we could hear him say, "Be careful, little men. I like the nightshift to be nice and quiet. You don't want to upset Carl."

Carl's enormous hand reached in the door to slap down on the switch on the wall and the lights were turned out again. Everything about that guy gave me the creeps. He was a big creep. He made my skin crawl.

I laid in my bed staring at the blank ceiling, trying hard to remember what it was that I was dreaming about and what woke me up so abruptly … but I couldn't. Then, I heard Timmy whispering something to me. "Hey, Marvin. Marvin, are you still awake over there?"

Trying to keep our voices as low as possible, I whispered back, "Yeah, I'm still awake. What's up, Timmy?"

He asked, "Do you really not remember your nightmare or were you just saying that in front of Carl to shut him up?"

"No, I really can't remember it. I'm trying to figure it out but I don't have a clue. I can remember the blood. That's all."

Timmy turned on his side, facing me, as he confessed, "I hate everything about this place so much. I just hate being locked inside here. Just the fact that I'm trapped here in this hellhole gives me nightmares."

I guess he turned on his side so he could be heard a little more easily. I agreed. "You know, I don't like it here either. My parents don't even come here to see me. Dr. Dunlap told me that my parents called him and said it was too far for them to drive here."

Timmy bellowed, "That's nothing, Marvin. I haven't seen my parents in almost three years. So, beat that. One time, Dunlap took me out of here and put me into a foster care house instead of letting me go home to be with my real family. Why would he do that to me?"

I questioned, "Do you think that's what he's going to do to me? I'd never see my parents or Kent again. That'd be a horrible thing."

Timmy paused for a moment before he said, "Maybe and maybe not. I suppose it all depends on what your family says and how well you do in here. You know … your progress."

I told Timmy that I was doing everything they asked me to. Then, came a dead silence before Timmy decided to spill his guts to me. "Sometimes,

I get so afraid here."

I told him I felt that way too before he added, "Once in a while, I think that I just want to kill myself."

"Kill yourself?"

Timmy nodded. "I actually thought about it so many times but I wouldn't know how to pull it off. Most of the time I hate even being alive. Do you ever feel that way, Marvin?"

I thought about it for a minute but didn't give him an answer. He added, "In here, I'd bet we all feel that way eventually."

I don't think I ever thought about killing myself. So, I didn't understand Timmy's way of thinking. I questioned, "Why? Why do you feel that way, Timmy?"

"Because, Marvin, some of us … no … every one of us, gets tired of the medications and the groups and the voices and the dull yellow walls in every room. It never seems to get any better in here … and, I believe that the longer you stay here, the crazier you're going to get. That's just how I feel, Marvin."

Wow, that was a mouthful. Timmy was certainly telling me how it was, how he felt. Up until then he was usually quiet and reserved and basically kept to himself. But why now? Why was he giving me his insight on the asylum now? Did he notice something different about me? Was I starting to act crazier than they said I actually was? I told him, "They told me I'd only be in a locked unit for a little while. Then, they said we all end up going to a better unit. Unit 11."

He chuckled quietly, "That's so funny, Marvin. That's what they told all of us. I've been on this unit for over six months … this time around. Charlotte has been here for nearly a year. The others have been stuck in here even longer than that." I watched as Timmy turned onto his back and stared at the ceiling for a moment before he rolled back on his side to face me again.

I stated, "Nearly a year … or longer? I don't think my parents would allow them keep me locked in here for that long."

I pondered if they'd do that to me. I mean, they were the ones who brought me here in the first place. They were the ones who dropped me off and never even bothered to say goodbye or come back for a visit. They were the ones who said that the drive was too far for them to go for a visit. It made me wonder. Was I going to be stuck in Unit 3 for six months or a year, or longer?

Timmy said, "Think about it, Marvin. We're all trapped in here and we can't get out. This is a prison, not a hospital."

Once again, he rolled over on his back and

put his hands up behind his head as if he were laying on a soft green lawn in the summertime, staring up at the constellations. I said nothing. He added, "Then, we have that horrible jerk Carl. I just want you to know that you shouldn't trust him. He's not a nice guy."

"What do you mean? What do you know about Carl?" I wondered how we suddenly moved onto the topic of Carl.

"He'll hurt you if you don't do what he wants you to do. He has no problem hitting kids our size. He even hits the girls. I've even seen him slap Charlotte around a lot."

I was puzzled. I asked, "What does he want us to do?"

"Different things, Marvin. All kinds of things. Things I can't talk about but you'll find out sooner or later."

There was a moment of dead silence before he added, "If you don't do what he wants, I swear, he'll hurt you really bad."

This was the first time I was hearing stuff about Carl. I probed, "Can't you just go to one of the nurses or Dr. Dunlap and tell them what he's doing to you?"

"A few of the kids have tried to do that but it always ends up the exact same way. Carl just tells Dunlap and the nurses that you're delusional and they end up increasing your meds until you're even more zombie-like than you were before. You end up like Harry." Then, there was another brief pause of silence.

Timmy admitted, "Now, I just do whatever he says to do and most of the time I close my eyes, pretend I'm not there and wait for it all to be over. That's usually when I wish I was dead. That's why I wish I was dead."

I still couldn't remember the nightmare that had me so wired that night or was it a sign of things to come? I hated it when I'd forget things. I could only remember the blood.

And then I was trapped in another endless session with Dunlap. His questions were stupid and pointless. They were the same questions he asked me before. So, I gave him the same answers that I did before.

Looking in the file, he said, "Let's talk about your nightmares, Marvin."

"I told you. I can't remember any of those nightmares."

Looking back in the files, he said, "Let's talk about your brothers, Marvin."

"I don't like talking about them. They're not important to me."

Staring into that damned file again, he said,

"Let's talk about your episodes of bedwetting, Marvin."

"I have accidents once in a while. It's really no big deal."

Laying the file down on the desk, he glared over at me and said, "Let's talk about your facial tick, Marvin."

"Facial tick? What are you talking about? I don't have a facial tick." When did my cheek start twitching like that?

Blah. Blah. Blah. We talked about the same things over and over and over. We talked every one of those senseless topics to death. It was one stupid session after miserable session and it seemed that nothing was ever getting accomplished. I wasn't getting anywhere. I wasn't doing any better. I was the same as I'd always been.

I felt like I'd been in that damned asylum forever. My summer vacation was going straight to hell and still no word from Mom or Dad … that I knew about. I came to the realization that they had simply forgot about me. They dumped me off in that place and went on with their lives. I'd been there for way too long.

"Marvin, did you hear my question? Marvin, did you hear me?"

Like I really wanted to hear his monotone questions. I played along and spoke politely. "No, I didn't. I was thinking about something else. Sorry, Dr. Dunlap".

Dunlap scolded me. "You have to stay focused in our sessions or I won't be able to help you!"

I lowered my head but didn't say a word to him as he continued. "You continually seem to wander off into your daydreams, Marvin. I need to have your undivided attention. This isn't a game we're playing."

I didn't think it was a game. He seemed to get even angrier when I didn't try to defend my actions. "It's all very, very serious. If you ever plan on getting out of here, you have to wake up and stop acting like a spoiled brat!"

I was flabbergasted. I never heard him get so mad with me. I knew it was time to apologize to him or I'd be stuck in his office for another freaking hour. I told him again and again, "I'm really sorry, Dr. Dunlap. I'm just very tired. My meds make me so tired."

He replied, "By now, you should be used to your medications. They shouldn't be bringing on such drowsy side effects."

How was I supposed to get used to being drugged against my will? "I'm used to them … well … sort of used to them. But I'm still a little bit hazy and confused a lot of the time." I tried my best to explain this feeling to him.

Without any concern for what I just told him, he opened that dammed file and peered inside it. "Shall we continue?"

I nodded my head and gave him a half-smile. Exhausted and defeated, I answered, "Sure, Dr. Dunlap. Let's continue."

He added, "And please, young man, try to stay focused this time". Then, he gave me one of his famous winks.

He stood up from his chair and walked around the desk. He sat on its edge, right in front of me. "Why don't we talk about something a little different today … change it up a bit."

Finally, we were getting somewhere. He wanted to talk about something different. I nodded my head.

"How about we discuss your three sisters? You don't usually mention their names. I wonder why that is."

Why did we have to talk about them? None of them ever tried to contact me in here. Besides, I wasn't really close to any of them. They'd hang out at Charlie's Pizza Place with their cool friends or go and run off with their boyfriends. I questioned him, "What about them?"

"Your sisters names are Jeannie, Sheila and Jodie. Is that correct?"

This conversation was useless. Why was he asking me their names when I knew he had it all printed out on the information chart in that damned folder. All he had to do was look down and read it. But, I gave in and answered him just to move the session along. "Yes, that's their names, Dr. Dunlap … Jeannie, Sheila and Jodie."

And once again, question after question about other people and how I got along with them. He never bothered to ask how any of them treated me. I knew it! I was never getting out of that place. Timmy was right. I was going to be trapped in that hellhole for the rest of my life.

I left my meeting with Dunlap and saw Evan sitting in a chair outside his office. He was waiting for the next appointment.

"Hey, Evan."

"Hey, Marvin. How did it go in there? Did he bore you to tears?"

"It was just as stupid as always. He asks me the dumbest questions."

Evan chuckled, "I know what you mean, Marvin. I never get anywhere in my one on ones with Dr. Dunlap."

"It's such a waste of my time and he always makes me late for lunch."

"He just doesn't know when enough is enough."

"Did you already eat lunch?"

"Yeah. Yours is still up there waiting for you. It was pretty bad today."

"What did we have?"

"Fish sticks. They tasted like little pieces of cardboard. I only ate two of mine."

I gave Evan a smile and said, "I'll see you later on in group."

He nodded. "Okay, Marvin."

Most of the time, Nurse Lisa or Nurse Noreen ran the different groups, so they weren't that bad. Having Lisa there instead of one of those fat and nasty nurses was a big plus. And, like every other day of the week, everyone sat in a big circle in the center of the meeting room.

We had groups that addressed socialization skills, cleanliness and hygiene, relaxation therapy, arts and crafts, exercise, and whatever new things they'd decide to throw at us each week. It made the time go by a little faster.

I recall one afternoon in the socialization group. Timmy, Charlotte, Andrew, Rick, Paulette, Evan and Anita were there. But that was the day that I didn't see Harry being wheeled in. It was odd. I'd never known Harry to miss any group. I supposed that he must have been sick or in with the doctor. Where did Harry go?

We had a new girl visiting the unit. Lisa said to her, "I'd like you to introduce yourself to the rest of the group."

The tall, thin girl with brown curly hair and dark glasses stood there and nervously stated, "I'm Marci … Wilcox."

It was as if the girl suddenly forgot her own last name. She and I made total eye contact for a split second.

I decided to take control and introduce myself before Lisa asked me to. I raised my hand and announced, "Hello Marci. Welcome to Unit 3. I'm Marvin, Marvin Skinner".

I noticed that Lisa seemed quite pleased that I took the initiative to make Marci feel comfortable. Then, I gave Marci a considerate smile as a way to let her know she wasn't stuck in that place alone. I could see the relief in her eyes.

Lisa pointed to an empty orange, plastic chair. "You can have a seat over there, Marci." She sat down quietly.

Timmy, seated next to me, elbowed me in the side and nodded toward Marci. Then, he leaned in and whispered, "Another unwilling guest trapped in the nuthouse."

After the meeting, we all went back to our separate rooms. Timmy got into his bed and said he was going to take a nap before dinner. I could feel the meds kicking in, so I decided to do the same. I never remember sleeping this much until I came to this place.

I didn't see Harry all day. He wasn't in the rec room for dinner either. Later, I got up the nerve to ask Carl what happened to Harry. He smiled and remarked, "Lucky kid got to go home. His family broke him out early this morning before any of you brats got out of bed. I hope he never has to come back here again."

I was thrilled for Harry and for myself too. Someone finally got out of there. It made me think that maybe I'd be next. Maybe mom and dad would come for me sooner or later. If that was the case, I'd still have at least part of my summer vacation left to be a bum and have some fun down at the arcade. It gave me great hope.

Another week passed me by and nothing … absolutely nothing … same groups, same doctor visits, same medications. No sunlight. No parents. No nobody.

Whenever we had a break from our, so called, structured environment, Timmy and I started hanging out with Marci a lot. She was a little more upbeat than the rest of the kids on the unit. That's probably because Dr. Dunlap hadn't adjusted her medications yet. She seemed to be so happy and content all the time. I couldn't imagine why she was even there with us in the first place.

Then, at our relaxation therapy group that morning, I glanced around the room and noticed that Evan wasn't attending.

Lisa put her hand up, as we all stared around the room, and said, "Before you ask me where Evan is, I wanted to let you know that he won't be at any more of our groups. Happily, he graduated out of Unit 3 and was transferred up to Unit 11 early this morning."

I glimpsed around the room and saw how small the group was, only seven of us. I leaned into Timmy, bumped his elbow and whispered, "You were up before me. Did you see Evan leaving the unit this morning?"

"No, I didn't see anyone. But I wish it was me. I'm so tired of this unit and, from what I hear, Unit 11 is the best unit they have in this place. A long time ago, Lisa told me that in Unit 11 you don't have to take medications or go to sessions with the doctor."

Chubby, blonde Anita, who I'd never really spoken too much to, leaned in from the other side. "I heard they have wonderful food in Unit 11. They even say the kids there are free to walk around the grounds whenever they want to. That's the unit I want to go to."

I responded, "Really? That sounds so much better than this place, Anita."

She remarked, "That's exactly where I want to be. I'm so tired of all these medications they have me taking."

Another girl, sitting next to Anita, said, "I should be the next one o go to Unit 11. I made more progress than anyone else here." She didn't wait for us to respond. She just crossed her arms and stared ahead.

Later that day, I had to meet with good old Dunlap and Nurse Greta to have my weekly blood tests done. This was how he evaluated my meds to figure out if they needed to be adjusted. I guessed that was just something they had to do every now and then in crazy houses.

As I sat there with a cotton ball taped to my arm, Dunlap asked me another series of strange questions. He asked me again if I had remembered any of the nightmares that I'd been experiencing recently.

I tried to think back but I got nothing. He grilled me and told me to think harder. He said I wasn't even trying. It was almost as if he thought I was lying to him. He was determined to pull all that information out of me, but I couldn't recall any of the nightmares. I observed him as he scribbled more things down in my file.

After an hour, he called Lisa to come to the office and retrieve me. When she arrived there, he told her that he was going to increase two of my medications. Great! That meant even more sleeping and confusion.

As I was leaving his office, I saw Andrew standing at the door, waiting to see the doctor after me. I never really had much to say to Andrew. He was a lot like Charlotte … overmedicated and in a zombie-like state. They even had the same shuffle when they walked.

While I was walking down the depressing pale-yellow hallway, I could hear Dunlap opening his door and saying, "Hello, Andrew, and how are you today? Come in and have a seat. We have a lot of work today."

A lot of days and weeks had gone by and Dunlap's new medication schedule had me even more screwed up. I felt so much worse than I did before. It was as if I couldn't think for myself anymore. I just did whatever they told me to do … like a trained dog … like Charlotte … and Andrew … but it was all in slow motion.

I remember the day that I walked up to the nurses' station and asked fat and old Nurse Susan, "Excuse me, Nurse Susan. Do you know what day it is today?"

She seemed a little bothered that I even spoke to her. She shrugged her shoulders but then responded, "Today is Thursday, Marvin. Today is Thursday."

I knew it was Thursday. That's not what I meant to ask her. I clarified it. "No, Nurse Susan. What month and day is it?"

She glanced down at her little desk calendar and said, "Oh, it's … ah … July 22nd. Why did you want to know that?"

I hung my head and mumbled, "No reason, Nurse Susan. I just wondered," as I realized I'd been entombed in that crazy house for over two months. I still hadn't heard one word from my Mom or Dad. I wondered if they were still too busy with their jobs and looking after my siblings, that they just forgot I was here.

As I stood at the end of the hall, Marci and Timmy approached to tell me that Rick was moved to Unit 11 that same morning. How could Rick have been moved to the Unit 11 when he never made one ounce of progress in the whole time I was there? I believed that I made a hundred times more progress than he did.

I noticed how small our groups had gotten to be. They were getting smaller every week. Now, it was just me, Timmy, Marci, Paulette, Anita,

Andrew and Charlotte. I wanted to be the next one to leave.

It was as if everyone else was leaving there for Unit 11 and new foster homes but not me. And nobody new was ever coming in. Weren't there anymore crazy kids in America just waiting to be committed to the asylum?

About two weeks later, it had to have been the beginning of August, Andrew was suddenly released and taken home by his parents. At least, that's what we were told by Carl. Every release seemed to be a spur of the moment decision around that that place and everyone seemed to be moved first thing in the morning.

I wondered if that's how it would happen for me. One day soon, I'd be sitting in that miserable pale-yellow prison cell and then, the next very next second, my parents would be at the admissions office signing papers for my release. I hoped that's how things would have played out for me … and the others.

Some nights, I was awakened by weird noises that were coming from across the hall in Charlotte's room. There were grunting sounds and an occasional cry. I knew that the cry was coming from Charlotte but I didn't know why she had been sobbing … whimpering.

I remember the night that I mustered up the courage to find out what the hell was going on in there. I saw Timmy was still sound asleep in his bed. So, I quietly crept out of my bed and opened the door slowly and carefully. I watched and waited very quietly.

I must have been standing there for at least twenty minutes, maybe a half hour, listening to the grunts and the sobs, until I finally saw Carl creeping out of Charlotte's room. He was zipping up his white trousers and grinning. I knew exactly what that meant.

Carl was doing things to Charlotte that shouldn't have been done to a little girl. That explained why Charlotte was always so quiet and confused. It wasn't just the medications. It was Carl and his disgusting acts. He was the monster that Timmy said he was. I knew he was a creep but I didn't know just how much of a creep he was until that moment.

I observed as he meandered back down to the nurse's station. He slapped his hand down on the counter … proud of himself. That must have been a great triumph for him … gratified to know that he, a thirty-some year-old, six-foot-two man, could rape, Charlotte, a helpless, over-medicated, ten-year-old girl.

Nurse Diane glanced up at him, grimaced and asked, "Are you all done?"

Carl, still grinning, crossed his arms and replied, "All done and feeling fine."

I found it even more sickening when I realized Nurse Diane and, most likely, the other nurses in the unit knew what he was doing and didn't try to stop it.

The next day, Nurse Diane told us that the snotty girl, Paulette, was moved to Unit 11. It was all happening way too fast. Since I was placed in Unit 3, four of the boys and one of the girls were released but we never saw any of them actually leaving the floor. That was about the time I finally realized that something was wrong with Unit 3. I talked secretly with Timmy and Marci. They, in turn, talked to Charlotte and Anita about the whole situation.

Later that afternoon, we got together with Marci and she taught us a little trick she learned when she was living in a group home. She called it 'cheeking' her meds. All five of us started to do this. I didn't know how it'd work out since I never saw the other four kids off their meds. We were able successfully do this without Carl or the nurses noticing and, about a week later, we were all feeling a lot less confused. But, just to be on the safe side, we still pretended as if we were the overmedicated zombies that they were used to.

We weren't sleeping as much as we used to, so, we got to overhear more of the conversations between Carl, Diane, Lisa and the others. At night, Timmy and I would creep out of our beds and listen at the door. One night, we heard them talking. Carl giggled, "So, who's going to be next? Maybe we should just flip a coin."

Diane remarked, "Who cares, as long as it's one of them. One less little derelict for us to have to deal with."

Lisa stated, "Dr. Dunlap said it has to be either Timmy, Charlotte or Anita. They've been here the longest."

Timmy's eyes opened widely as he gasped and stared at me. We heard Carl add, "Whoever it is, I have to know for sure. Then, I can take them to Unit 11. If these kids had any idea of what Unit 11 really was, they be horrified. We have them all believing it's better than this place. Hell! If they only knew."

We heard the laughing and giggling and bullshitting for over an hour. I said to Timmy, "What did he mean when he said that if we knew what Unit 11 really was? I don't get it. They said Unit 11 was nicer than Unit 3. I guess they lied about that too."

Timmy bowed his head and commented, "I don't know if I could survive in a place that's even worse than here."

Then, I questioned, "But how much worse could it be?"

Timmy shrugged his shoulders before we went back to bed. He didn't sleep all night. Every time he heard the slightest noise, he thought it might be Carl coming to take him to Unit 11. I thought the same thing. Then, by one or two in the morning, we both drifted off to sleep from the pure exhaustion we were feeling.

When morning came Timmy was still in the bed across the room. I looked at him and whispered, "Oh no. What about Charlotte or Anita? Carl must have taken one of them."

We got up and went out to the dining area for breakfast and meds. Marci soon followed. We waited to see if Charlotte or Anita were going to join us but we didn't see either of them at first. A few minutes later, Anita emerged from the girls' bathroom.

I questioned Lisa where Charlotte was. She pointed down the hallway and stated, "Oh, the little sleepy head must have had a hard time waking up this morning. Here she comes now."

Charlotte was there, holding her little brown

teddy bear with the missing eye. Anita was there, smiling and eating cereal. Timmy was there but he was still a nervous wreck. Carl didn't take any of them to Unit 11 last night. Timmy and I questioned if we actually heard the conversation correctly. We didn't know.

The following night was a little different than what we had heard before. We listened at the door again but didn't hear anyone speaking. No one was joking or complaining or bullshitting. We must have stood there until after one o'clock in the morning and the entire unit was silent. It was an eerie haunting silence. That was around the time that we finally turned in.

Two hours later, I remember that I woke up kicking and screaming about blood again. I was completely covered in sweat. My pillow and my sheets were wet. I opened my eyes and saw Carl standing over my bed, just staring down at me with those crazy hollow eyes.

Diane walked into the room and sat down on the bed next to me. I observed as Carl made a quiet exit from the room. Diane said, "Are you alright, Marvin? It looks like you had another one of those nightmares again."

I nodded and murmured, "Yeah, I guess I did, Nurse Diane."

"Do you have any idea what this one was about? Was it about blood again?"

I couldn't remember. She tried to help calm me down until I rolled over and drifted off back to sleep again.

When morning rolled around and we came to get our meds, Charlotte wasn't there and Anita wasn't there either. Carl leaned over the nurses' station and told us, "Charlotte and Anita graduated from Unit 3 and were transferred to Unit 11 this morning. Isn't that great news?"

Something suddenly popped up in my mind. It was something I never noticed or questioned before. I asked Diane, "How come we haven't seen any new kids coming in here lately?"

She replied, "I guess we've just been putting all the new kids directly into Unit 11 instead of this unit. But don't worry, Marvin. I'm sure that you'll be going there sooner or later."

Carl, standing next to Diane, crossed his arms, smirked and mumbled, "Yeah. Hopefully, sooner than later."

I really hated that guy and his smug attitude. I knew Charlotte and Anita didn't go to Unit 11, or did they? Where the hell was Unit 11 anyway? I had to find out. My head was clearer and I could think again but those damned voices kept coming back and telling me to do bad things to people. It felt like they were stronger and louder than ever. Why were they back?

There were more meetings with Dunlap, more groups with Lisa and Diane, and even more threatening gestures and looks from weird Carl every night.

I began to worry about Timmy. He was here before Marci and I had arrived. All the kids that were there longer, disappeared first, so he would have been the next logical choice. We continued to 'cheek' our medications and pretend as if we were still taking them.

There was a point one evening when I asked Timmy and Marci to create a commotion down at the end of the hallway near the girl's bathroom so I could get into the nurses' station to see if I could get hold of a file.

They did exactly as we intended. Their acting was brilliant. The situation pulled Lisa and Diane to the end of the hallway for a good length of time. Luckily, Carl wasn't working that shift or he would've figured us out.

I crept down the hall and slipped quietly into the nurse's station unnoticed, but I was still able to see the end of the hallway from out of the corner of my eye.

I opened each of the desk drawers, trying not to shuffle any loose pens or pencils that might make noise. I didn't find any files in the desk. I turned to the gray, rusted cabinet behind me and began rummaging through it.

As I fingered through those damned manila folders, I found the three files that I was looking for. The tab on the first file was labeled Marvin Skinner. The other two files were labeled Marci Wilcox and Timothy Hart. I paged through each of the files and tried to read through them as quickly as possible, but I couldn't find out anything that I didn't already know.

Then, I discovered a curious page in each of our files. They were letters to our parents that told them we had all been placed in foster care group homes hundreds of miles away and that contact wasn't such a good idea at this time. What? We were all placed in the foster care system? We were hundreds of miles away? That never happened. It was no wonder I never heard a peep from my Mom or Dad. They were led to believe that I was already sent away from this crazy place. They were lied to, just like I was.

As I tried to get the folders back into the cabinet as quickly and quietly as I could, I noticed another drawer marked, 'Closed Patients'. I felt my heart beginning to beat faster and harder. Somehow,

I knew what I was about to see before I opened the drawer.

I carefully pulled the gray metal drawer open and removed the files that were labeled Anita Hale, Charlotte Stephens, Harold Smith, Richard Andros, Evan Michaels, Paulette Jackson and Andrew Morgan.

The list went on and on. I must have counted at least fifty more separate files in that one drawer alone. That was when it all came together in my head. It was as if a lightbulb came on and I could see what Unit 11 really was.

I placed all the files back exactly where I found them and snuck out of the nurse's station almost as easily as I got in. When Marci and Timmy saw me, they suddenly ended their rants, apologized to the nurses, and let Unit 3 return to normal. Well … normal for Unit 3.

I told them what I'd found out. We all knew that we had to find a way to escape from that place before we were moved into the Closed Patient files like the others.

We played along as best we could but it was getting harder and harder to not look suspicious while Marci and I watched out for Timmy. We knew we had to protect him because it was obvious that he'd be their next choice.

The next day, I got together with Timmy and Marci in the rec room. We sat on one of the worn tan sofas in the corner and kept our voices low enough that no one could hear. Marci began. "We have to get out of here before they take all of us to Unit 11."

I scratched my head. "I know we have to find a way out, but how? Everything's locked down and we don't have the keys to open anything. How are we going to get out?"

Timmy suggested, "We've been pretty good at sneaking around. Maybe one of us could get the keys from the nurses' station." Timmy and Marci looked at me.

I sat upright and crossed my arms. I couldn't believe what they were asking me to do again. "Oh no. I already broke into the files. It's someone else's turn."

Marci hinted, "What about Carl?"

"What about Carl?"

"He always has his set of keys hanging from his belt. It might be easier to get them from him if he took his pants off."

Timmy slapped his leg. "And why the hell would Carl take his pants off?"

Marci bowed her head and said, "He was taking them off when he visited Charlotte's room at night."

I realized what Marci was offering. There was no way we were going to use her as bate to be molested by that monster. "No way, Marci. He's not going to do that to you."

"But it might be the only way. I don't care what he does. It's not like it hasn't happened to me before."

I stopped. "You mean to tell me that you've been raped?"

She confessed, with tears in her eyes. "Yes. It was by one of my many foster fathers. I tried to tell my caseworker but she didn't believe me. She said I needed to stop lying about him and I should start acting more grateful. He did that to me almost every night for a year."

I put my hands up and said, "No, Marci. I'm not going to let him do that to you."

"Then, what do you suggest? I'm all out of ideas, Marvin."

"We'll figure something out. There has to be another way to get the keys."

"I just hope it's not too late when you figure it out."

We tried to come up with other plans on how to get those keys and get the hell out of that nuthouse. Every time we came up with an idea, one of us would say why the idea wouldn't work. We were banging our heads on the wall but nothing was making sense.

It was early September when it all came to a grinding halt. One night … it had to be around two in the morning when I heard the bedroom door creaking as it opened slowly. The room was dark but I could still see Carl's intimidating silhouette standing in the doorway.

He approached Timmy. As he got closer, Timmy woke up and started screaming at the top of his lungs. Carl wasn't expecting this. He was sure Timmy's medications would have had him sound asleep. He jumped back for a moment when Timmy surprised him with his alertness.

Then, Marci came running into our room screaming even louder than Timmy was. Diane and Lisa followed in soon after. They were astounded to see us all so awake and aware. Diane commented, "I knew it! I just had a feeling! You haven't been taking your medications. Have you? I can see it in your eyes."

I screamed loudly, "No, we haven't been taking them! So what?"

She added, "Every one of you are breaking the rules here!"

My rant continued when I revealed the truth. "We know all about the three of you! We know all about Unit 11 too!"

Carl rolled his eyes and chimed in with, "You don't know what you're talking about, you little bastard."

"You're not taking us there! You can't make us go there!"

"Shut up!" Just then, Carl slapped me across the face so hard I could feel the sting and the heat on my cheek as I tumbled off the bed and onto the dirty white tile floor below him.

He turned to Lisa and Diane and stated, "This is all really stupid. Keeping these brats is really stupid. Why are we even listening to this bullshit from a bunch of derelicts? I say we just take all three of them down to Unit 11 now and be done with it. Then, they won't be our problem anymore and we'll never have to see them again. I really hate these little bastards."

Lisa looked over at Diane, who nodded her head, and said, "All three, it's not our usual protocol but I'll give Dr. Dunlap a call and let him know what's going on."

I couldn't believe Lisa was part of this too. How could a beautiful woman like that be so damned disturbed? We watched as she picked up the phone and talked to Dunlap. He must have been giving her instructions on what to do with us. Carl stood there with his arms crossed. We just waited to see what was going to happen next.

"Yes, Randall. I know this is an unusual situation but it has to be done."

I listened to the conversation Lisa was having with Dr. Dunlap. It sounded as if she was trying to convince him to send us to that damned Unit 11."

"Unit 11 it is. No, I have Carl and Diane here to help me. Thank you, Randall. I'll see you in the morning."

Once she hung up the phone, Lisa became very aggressive. She grabbed Marci by the roots of her hair and pulled her out of the room. Marci fell to the floor and tried kicking Lisa. It didn't matter. Lisa just dragged her along. Diane took Timmy by the upper arm, and, of course, I was stuck with big and dumb Carl. He lifted me up and carried me out of the room.

We tried to fight back but they were much bigger and stronger than we were. They dragged us down the pale-yellow halls, down the elevator and out the front door.

After they made the three of us stumble through the pitch-dark grounds for about fifteen minutes, we finally arrived at our destination. Marci put her hands up to her mouth and began to cry hysterically. I watched as her body began to shake uncontrollably. Timmy stood there frozen in place gasping at the sight.

I stared ahead and saw a small wooden, hand-carved sign in front of me that read Unit 11. Just beyond the sign was a dark and eerie graveyard filled with little, wooden crosses to mark where each of the bodies were buried. There were no names on the crosses to identify who was buried in which plot but we knew there was one there for Harry and another for Anita and still another for poor little Charlotte.

I watched as Lisa took a straight-edged razor from her pocket and, in an instant, sliced Marci's throat. The young girl tried to make a noise, any kind of noise, but instead blood gurgled from her mouth and neck. She put her hands on her throat to try to stop the bleeding but it didn't help. In a few seconds, her eyes rolled back as she fell to the ground and landed facedown. I screamed, "Why! Why did you do that to her? She never did anything to you! She never hurt anyone!"

Lisa said, "You just don't get it, do you kid? Unit 3 is filled with the incurables, the unwelcome, the ridiculous and pathetic little bastards that no one wants anymore. Those are the kids who can never become productive adults and reenter society again. Our Unit 3 is the final stop for all of those young homicidal maniacs."

I didn't understand why Lisa was saying what she was saying to me, or did I? I tried to reason with her, "But I never killed anyone and neither did they."

Lisa was quick to inform us, "Sure you did. All of you did. This little bitch on the ground lit her house on fire one night and killed her two-year-old sister. At first, they thought it was an accident but later found out that it was deliberate. Marci was jealous of a two-year-old."

I shouted, "No! You're lying! Marci would never do that!"

She continued. "A few months after that, she stabbed at least five other children in her school cafeteria during lunch. So, don't tell me none of you ever killed anyone."

I stayed strong and barked, "I don't believe you, Lisa! After all, you're just Dunlap's little bitch, aren't you?"

She threw a wicked look at me. Then she stared at Timmy with contempt in her evil eyes. I screamed, "No! Not Timmy! He didn't kill anyone and neither did I!"

Lisa corrected me. "I guess you never heard the real truth, Marvin. Didn't Timmy ever tell you how he killed his own mother with a rope while she was sleeping … strangled her. After a year and a half of psychotherapy, Timmy was placed in a foster home where he did the exact same thing to his foster mother while she was asleep. He has a little problem with mother figures."

Timmy hollered out, "Don't listen to them, Marvin! It's not true! None of it is true! I never killed anyone! They're just trying to turn us against each other!"

Were they telling the truth? Even if Timmy and Marci did kill someone, I certainly didn't kill anyone or I would've remembered. I couldn't kill anyone.

I struggled to get free from Carl's powerful clutches as Lisa continued. "And you, Marvin, you killed your older brother Kent. You held a butcher knife up to his neck and you murdered him in cold blood. Don't you remember that?"

"I didn't kill my brother. I remember the day it happened but I know that I never even cut him. We were just fooling around and I just wanted to scare him."

Carl chimed in. "Oh, you killed him, you deranged little bastard. You shoved that knife so deep into his throat that you almost cut his head off."

I didn't remember any part of what they were telling me. Lisa added, "Then you killed the family dog."

I was so confused at that point. I couldn't recall if I did those things or if it was all just some great big lie to make me more confused than I already was. Of course, I did experience all those nightmares with blood. I wondered if the blood had something to do with Kent.

Diane was anxious and wanted to get back inside. "Enough of this crap. It's chilly out here and I'm freezing my ass off. Can we just finish what we started, Lisa?"

Lisa smiled and gave Diane a quick nod. I watched as Diane took a knife from her pocket and plunged the blade into Timmy's chest. He looked down at the knife sticking out of him and then looked at me with a resigned expression on his face. The expression turned into an expression of peace. A gush of blood spurted from his mouth before his eyes, like Marci's, rolled back in his head and he dropped to the ground next to her. Diane kicked him once to make sure he was dead.

I watched them, waiting for some kind of movement, hoping it was all just some kind of sick joke. Neither of them moved. Neither of them was breathing but I'm sure that their eyes were still wide open and staring at the ground.

I felt dizzy and nauseous as my head began to spin because I knew that there was only one more person left for them to take care of and send off to Unit 11.

I realized that was going to be my last summer vacation. It wasn't quite the vacation I planned on originally. I'd never get to say goodbye to my Mom or Dad or my siblings. I just wished I knew if I really killed my brother or if it was just something that the three of them made up. I guess I'd never know.

Once again, I glanced into the cemetery, at all of those little wooden crosses standing in a random order. I could feel a river of uncontrollable tears streaming down my cheeks.

Carl grunted and said, "You're not so tough anymore, kid. Are you?"

I gazed up at the sign for Unit 11 again and realized there was no other way. I couldn't fight all three of them. My only allies were dead on the ground in front of me or already buried in that tiny cemetery.

In that moment, I recalled the faces of my Mom and Dad and my brother. The nightmares all came back to me and I realized that I was the one who ended Kent's life.

I stared at Diana and saw an evil desire in her eyes. I turned and focused on Lisa but her eyes were vacant and unemotional.

For the first time ever, Carl seemed to be quiet and respectful as he placed his big smelly hands on each side of my head. The last thing I felt was his hands twisting my head and the sound of a loud snap.

Made in the USA
Middletown, DE
09 January 2022

58234562R00047